Ponies on Parade

Do you love ponies? Be a Pony Pal!

Ponies on Parade

Jeanne Betancourt

Illustrated by Richard Jones

A
LITTLE APPLE
PAPERBACK

SCHOLASTIC INC.

New York Toronto London Auckland Sydney
Mexico City New Delhi Hong Kong Buenos Aires

ISBN 0-439-55988-X

12 11 10 9 8 7 6 5 4 3   5 6 7 8/0

Printed in the U.S.A.   40
First printing, September 2003

Contents

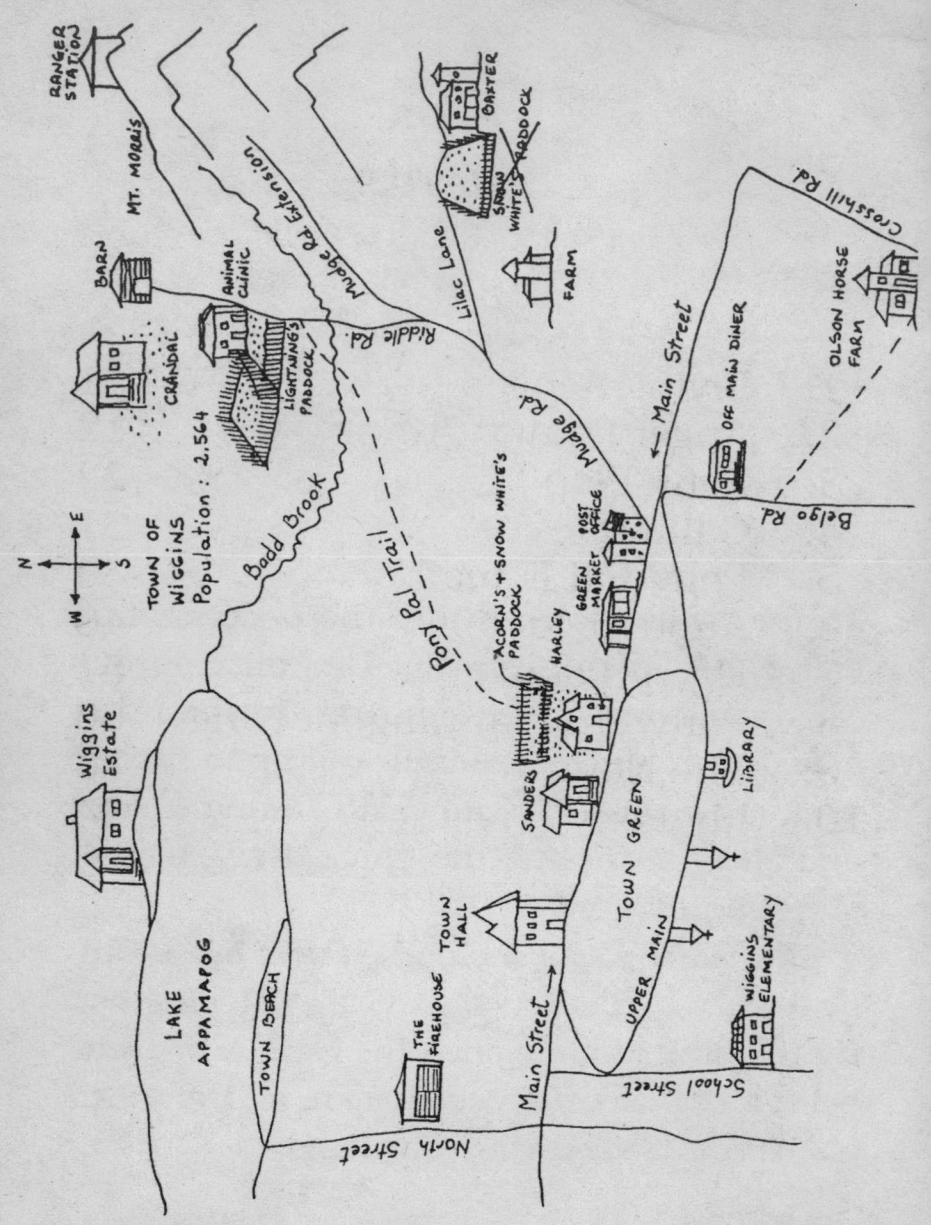

Flying Acorns

Anna Harley walked into the paddock and called her pony's name. The mischievous Shetland pony turned and ran to the other side of the paddock. Acorn was up to his old trick of playing "hard to catch." Anna turned and headed toward the gate. "Bye, Acorn!" she shouted.

After a few steps she peeked over her shoulder. Acorn had stopped and was watching her. By the time Anna opened the gate, Acorn was behind her. She turned quickly and grabbed his halter. "Fooled you!" she laughed.

Acorn didn't care. He was busy sniffing her jacket pocket for a treat. Anna pulled out an apple and gave it to him.

"Snow White," Anna called to the pretty Welsh pony in the middle of the paddock. "I have an apple for you, too." Snow White trotted over for her treat.

"Lulu will come out later," she told the ponies. "Then we'll all go for a trail ride."

Anna's Pony Pals, Lulu and Pam, were both home working on their research papers for school. "Pick something from your everyday life," Mrs. Waters had instructed. "Learn all you can about it and write a three-page paper."

I don't even have an idea for my paper, thought Anna. Pam and Lulu will finish before I even start mine.

Anna hated homework, especially when it meant she had to do a lot of reading or writing. Anna was dyslexic, so reading and writing were hard for her. She had to do both for the research paper. And worst of all, it was due on Tuesday. She'd had two weeks to work on it. Now she only had two days.

Anna sat on the fence and opened her notebook to a blank page.

If I just think hard enough, I'll come up with an idea, she decided. Anna looked up. Snow White and Acorn were sniffing each other's faces. It was so cute that she had to draw it. An hour later, Anna was on her third drawing of the ponies.

"Hey, Anna," Lulu called as she walked through the gate. "Ready to go trail riding? Or do you want to work on your paper a little longer?"

Anna closed her notebook. "I'm done for now," she said as she jumped down from the fence. "Let's saddle up." She didn't tell Lulu she was drawing, not writing.

Anna and Lulu rode along Pony Pal Trail to meet Pam and her chestnut-colored pony, Lightning. Pony Pal Trail was a mile-and-a-half woodland trail connecting Acorn and Snow White's paddock with the Crandals' property. Pam and Lightning were waiting for their Pony Pals by three birch trees. It was their favorite meeting spot.

Lulu brought Snow White to a halt next to Lightning. "I finished my paper about Mount Morris," she bragged. "It's *five* pages long. Now all I have to do is make sure there aren't any mistakes."

"I almost finished mine, too," announced Pam. "I learned so much about ballpoint pens. They used to leak like crazy." She turned to Anna. "What are you writing about?"

"It's a surprise," answered Anna. She was embarrassed that she didn't have an idea. She didn't want her friends to know. "I can't wait for the Fall Festival," she said to change the subject.

"That reminds me," said Pam. "I have some great news about the festival."

"What?" asked Lulu.

"Tell us," insisted Anna.

"I'll *show* you when we stop for a break," said Pam. She grinned at Anna. "You're going to love it."

"So where are we going to ride?" asked Anna.

"Let's ride the trails along Badd Brook," suggested Pam.

"And stop near the waterfall," said Lulu. "I can't wait to *see* your news."

It was Anna's turn to lead. When she was trail riding, she could forget all her school troubles. And she loved being first, with no one in front of her and her pony.

Half an hour later the ponies were drinking from Badd Brook. The girls sat on rocks nearby.

"So what's the surprise about the Fall Festival?" asked Anna.

Pam pulled a flyer out of her pocket and showed it to Anna and Lulu. "Someone just donated ten life-size pony statues to Wiggins," she explained. "There's a contest to

see who gets to paint them. The painted ponies will be auctioned off. It's a way to raise money for the fire department."

Anna and Lulu studied the flyer.

PONIES ON PARADE

You can paint a life-size pony!

Pick up applications at the town library
Draw your design in the pony outlines

Applications due:	**Tuesday, October 14**
Winners announced:	**Friday, October 17**
Ponies delivered:	**Saturday, October 18**

Paints and brushes donated by Klein's Hardware

PAINTED PONIES WILL BE ON PARADE
AT THE FALL FESTIVAL

SATURDAY, OCTOBER 25

AUCTION OF PAINTED PONIES AT 3:00 P.M.

All Fall Festival and Ponies on Parade
proceeds will go to the Wiggins Volunteer Fire Department.

"This is great," said Lulu enthusiastically.

"They had painted cows in New York City," said Pam. "I saw it on television. There was Americow the Beautiful and Cownt Dracula."

Lulu pointed to the flyer. "You have to do this, Anna," she said.

Anna tried to imagine painting a life-size pony. So far she'd only painted on paper. "I don't know," she said. "It sounds really hard."

"You can do it," insisted Pam.

"You're a great artist," added Lulu.

"I guess I could try," agreed Anna.

Pam picked up a flat stone and skimmed it across the water. The stone bounced twice before it sank. "The Fall Festival is always so much fun," she said. "Those painted ponies will make it even more fun."

Lulu skimmed a stone. Hers bounced three times. "It'll be tasty, too," she said. "Hot cider, doughnuts, and caramel-covered apples. Yum."

Pam's next skipping stone bounced three times. "And we'll give pony rides," she added. "On our *real* ponies."

Anna picked up a stick and drew an outline of a pony in the dirt. What kind of design could she put on a pony? The application was due on Tuesday. Her stomach turned over. The research paper was also due Tuesday. Two things due and zero ideas.

Something whizzed past Anna's head and dropped into the middle of the pony she was drawing. Anna picked up an acorn and showed it to Pam and Lulu.

"It almost hit me," she said. "Where'd it come from?"

Pam looked up and pointed. "It must have fallen from that oak tree," she said.

Anna glanced around at the ground. "There *are* a lot of acorns," she observed.

"Ouch!" shouted Pam. She rubbed her upper arm. "One hit me."

Another acorn fell in the water in front of Lulu.

Anna turned around. The acorns weren't coming from above them. They were coming from the woods. Someone was throwing them.

The Pony Pals exchanged a glance. "Tommy and Mike," they whispered.

Tommy Rand and Mike Lacey were eighth-grade boys who played tricks on the Pony Pals and teased them. Sometimes the boys did things that were dangerous. Like the time they stole the girls' ponies.

Suddenly, Snow White whinnied in surprise and reared up. "They hit Snow White!" exclaimed Lulu.

"Hey, man, you hit one of the ponies," said a boy's voice from the woods. Anna knew for sure that it was Mike Lacey's.

"Mike Lacey and Tommy Rand!" she yelled. "Stop it right now. You could really hurt someone."

"Or a pony," added Lulu angrily.

There was a scurrying sound in the woods.

"I think they're leaving," said Pam. "They probably have their bikes."

Anna was already pulling down her stirrups. "Hurry," she said. "We can catch them."

Pam held up her hand. "No," she said.

"They might throw more acorns. A pony could startle and throw one of us."

"Pam's right," agreed Lulu. She rubbed Snow White's flank. "It's too dangerous."

"But we can't let them get away with it," protested Anna.

"We won't," said Pam.

"We'll get back at them," agreed Lulu.

Anna knew Lulu and Pam meant what they said. But how will we do it? she wondered. And when?

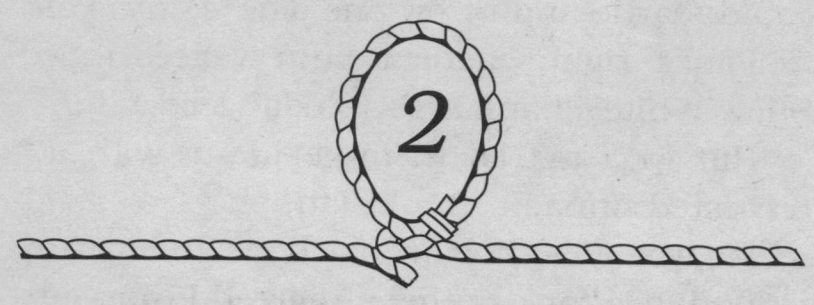

Angel Pony

Lulu and Anna sneaked into the woods to make sure the boys were gone.

Lulu pointed to the ground. "Lots of tire marks going east," she said.

Anna checked the trail going in the other direction. "No tire marks here," she said.

"So they must have gone back the way they came," observed Pam.

"Let's go the other way," suggested Lulu.

"We'll go right by Ms. Wiggins's house," said Anna. "We can tell her about Ponies on Parade."

Ms. Wiggins owned a big estate with a lot of wonderful riding trails. The Pony Pals could ride there whenever they wanted.

"Ms. Wiggins is a great artist," said Lulu.

"Just like you, Anna," added Pam.

Pam and Lulu think I'm such a good artist, thought Anna. I just hope I come up with an idea for painting a pony. I don't want to disappoint my best friends.

Anna thought about her Pony Pals as she rode behind them. She met Pam Crandal on the first day of kindergarten. During art class, the teacher said they could draw whatever they wanted. Anna drew a pony. Pam loved Anna's drawing and told her that she had a real pony. Anna also learned that Pam's father was a veterinarian and her mother was a riding teacher. Pam discovered that Anna's mother owned Off-Main Diner.

"I love the brownies there," Pam had said.

"My mom makes them," Anna had bragged.

Soon the two pony lovers were best friends.

Anna and Pam didn't meet Lulu Sanders until they were all ten years old. That was when Lulu moved to Wiggins. Lulu's father was a naturalist who traveled all over the world studying wild animals. Lulu's mother died when she was little. After that, Mr. Sanders took Lulu on his business trips. They traveled all over the world together. But when Lulu turned ten, Mr. Sanders said she should stay in one place. That's when Lulu moved to Wiggins to live with her grandmother Sanders.

Lulu thought living in Wiggins would be boring. Then she found Snow White and met Anna and Pam. Snow White became her pony and Anna and Pam became her Pony Pals.

Now the three best friends rode across the field toward Ms. Wiggins's house.

Pam turned in the saddle and called back to Anna and Lulu, "I see her. She's on the porch."

The girls tied their ponies to the hitching post near the barn and ran over to the house. Ms. Wiggins was sitting at a table with watercolor paints, brushes, and paper. She looked up and smiled at the girls.

"I'm so happy to see you," she said. "Have you heard about Ponies on Parade?"

"We were going to tell you about it," laughed Anna.

"I already have an idea," said Ms. Wiggins. She showed them a page of drawings. "Can you tell what it is?"

"It's an angel pony!" exclaimed Anna.

"I love it," said Lulu.

"It's wonderful," added Pam.

"I was thinking of Winston when I painted it," Ms. Wiggins explained.

Anna remembered Ms. Wiggins's old gray Shetland pony. The Pony Pals and Acorn were with him the night he died.

"Winston would definitely be an angel pony," said Lulu softly.

Ms. Wiggins nodded in agreement. Then

she smiled at Anna. "You should design one, too, Anna," she said. She pulled a few papers out of a folder. "I made copies of the application. You can have some."

"Thanks," said Anna as she took the papers.

That night, Anna sat at her desk and thought of ideas for a painted pony. Her first idea was a devil pony.

She didn't like it.
Next, she did a pony with stripes.

She didn't like that one, either. It looked too much like a zebra.

She was turning the stripes into a plaid pattern when her mother came into the room. "Anna, do you have a research paper due on Tuesday?" she asked.

"Yes," admitted Anna.

"What are you writing about?" Mrs. Harley asked.

"I can't decide," confessed Anna.

"Lulu's grandmother tells me you girls have had two weeks to do this assignment," she said. "Lulu is writing about Mount Morris."

Anna noticed that her mother had a new haircut. Lulu's grandmother was a hairdresser — the only one in Wiggins. And she loved to brag about Lulu.

Mrs. Harley leaned over the desk and picked up the half-plaid, half-striped pony drawing. "What's this?" she asked.

Anna started to explain about Ponies on Parade. But her mother didn't let her finish.

"A poster went up in the diner today," she said. "I wanted you to try out." She sighed. "That was before I heard about the paper. Your schoolwork is more important, Anna.

You may *not* work on the pony project until you've written that paper."

"But —" Anna began.

"No buts," her mother scolded. "Schoolwork has to come first."

Anna put her art supplies away. As her mother left, Anna took her books out of her backpack. Just looking at the gray three-ring binder made her feel stupid. And tired. She glanced at her watch. It was already 9:30. She'd go to bed now, get up early, and work on the paper all day tomorrow.

The next morning, Anna woke up to someone tickling her cheek. She opened her eyes and saw Lulu leaning over her. "Time to get up, sleepyhead," Lulu said softly. "It's a beautiful day and we're going for a trail ride. I called Pam."

Anna sat up and blinked. The sunlight was pouring into her room. It *was* a beautiful day.

"You get dressed and eat," said Lulu. "I'll saddle up our ponies. I already fed them."

Anna's mother was in the kitchen when

Anna came downstairs. "Where are you going?" she asked.

"For a ride," answered Anna.

"I thought we agreed that you'd work on that paper all day today," her mother said.

Anna had forgotten all about the paper — again.

"Please let me go," begged Anna. "Acorn needs exercise. I'll just ride for an hour. Then I'll come right back and work."

Her mother looked at the clock over the refrigerator. "Be back here by eleven," she said. "Not a minute after. And the rest of the day you stay in and write. Agreed?"

"Agreed," repeated Anna. She grabbed a banana and ran out the door before her mother changed her mind.

Lulu and Anna rode Pony Pal Trail to the Crandals'. Pam and Lightning were waiting for them.

"Where do you want to ride today?" asked Pam.

Anna was going to tell Pam and Lulu she could only ride for a little while. But Lulu spoke up first. "Let's go to Mount Morris," she said. "It'll be fun after I wrote about it."

"That's a great idea," exclaimed Pam. "We can ride through Morristown, too. We haven't been there in a long time."

Morristown was an abandoned town at the foot of Mount Morris. There were crumbling stone walls and fences where houses, barns, and farm fields used to be. The Pony Pals loved to explore the old ghost town. Riding to Mount Morris would take longer than an hour. But Anna didn't care. She was having too much fun.

Lulu and Snow White took the lead as they turned onto Riddle Road. Pam and Lightning followed. Anna and Acorn took up the rear.

When they reached Morristown Trail, Anna heard a noise in the woods behind her. She turned and saw a flash of red between the trees. Next, she saw the tail end of a bike. Tommy Rand and Mike Lacey were following them *again.*

Pony Plop

As soon as the trail widened, Anna pulled Acorn up beside Snow White.

"Mike and Tommy are following us," she whispered to Lulu. "Don't let them know we know."

Next, Anna rode up to Pam and told her the news.

"It's time for an emergency meeting," Pam whispered back.

Anna nodded. She knew it was also time for her to use her acting skills. "Where should we go next, Pam?" Anna asked in a loud voice.

"Let's ask Lulu," Pam said cheerfully. She winked at Anna to let her know she was acting, too.

The three girls moved their ponies into a circle. They made plans for the rest of their trail ride. But in between, they had a whispered meeting about the boys.

"We have got to lose them," said Pam. "They might throw things again."

"I saw this old cave on a map of Mount Morris," Lulu said. "I think I can find it."

Anna and Pam exchanged a smile. They knew that Mike and Tommy would be interested in a cave.

"We'll lead them there," continued Lulu. "They'll think we went inside."

"When they're in the cave, we'll take off," added Anna. "It's perfect."

"I can't wait to get to the *cave*," Anna shouted in her best acting style.

"It's the best cave," said Lulu. "It'll make a

perfect hideout. There's room for our ponies, too."

"Going in there will be so much fun," added Pam.

Pam and Lulu are good actresses, too, thought Anna.

Lulu took the lead. Pam came next. Anna and Acorn took up the rear. Anna heard a little scuffling sound in the woods behind her. But she didn't turn around once. She didn't want the boys to know that she knew they were there.

There were lots of turns in the trail. And twice Lulu had to choose whether to go left or right.

Finally, the Pony Pals came to an open stretch of trail.

"I remember this from the map," Lulu called back to Pam and Anna. "We're almost there. Let's ride full-out."

Good, thought Anna. The boys won't be able to keep up with us now. We'll get to the cave first.

When the trail split in two, Lulu made a

sharp right. The girls rode into a clearing and faced the cave.

Lulu halted Snow White in front of the opening. "Wow!" she said. "It's big. We really could ride our ponies in there."

As Anna pulled Acorn up next to Snow White, he raised his tail and dropped a pony plop. Right at the mouth of the cave.

"Perfect," said Lulu as she dismounted. "Acorn left a clue for Tommy and Mike. It looks like we took our ponies into the cave."

"We better hide before those guys get here," whispered Pam.

The girls quickly led their ponies into the woods near the cave.

"Be quiet now, Acorn," Anna whispered in her pony's ear.

Acorn nodded as if he understood.

The girls couldn't see the boys, but they could hear them coming.

"Hey, man," said Mike. "Why'd we have to keep following them?"

"Because we want to mess up their stupid little Pony Pest day," answered Tommy.

"We'll go in the cave and make ghost noises. That'll freak them out. Then it can be *our* hideout. Get it?"

"Tom, don't step in the —" Mike warned.

The next thing the girls heard was Tommy hollering.

Anna covered her mouth so she wouldn't laugh out loud.

"Sh-sh," Mike warned Tommy. "They'll hear us."

"Come on," said Tommy. "Let's freak them out."

The Pony Pals slowly left their hiding place. From inside the cave they heard a distant ghostly, "Ooh-hh. Ooo-hhhh."

The boys' mountain bikes were leaning against the rock ledge.

Anna knew that the fancy red bike was Tommy's. She squatted beside it and let the air out of the tire.

"Hurry, Anna," said Lulu between giggles.

Anna mounted Acorn and followed Lulu and Pam away from the cave.

Lulu led them off the wide trail onto

a smaller one. After a short distance, she stopped. "They'll never find us here," she said as she dismounted.

Pam slid off Lightning. "I brought some sandwiches," she announced. "Peanut butter and jelly."

"Great," said Lulu. She held up a pack of juice boxes. "Apple juice."

Anna glanced at her watch. It was noon. Her mother had said to be home by eleven. She was already an hour late. It would take her another hour to ride back home.

Pam handed Anna a sandwich and Lulu handed her a juice.

If I say I have to go, she thought, I'll ruin everybody's fun.

While the girls ate, they talked about how they'd tricked Tommy and Mike. "Tommy will have to walk his bike," giggled Lulu.

"It'll take them forever to get home," added Anna. Suddenly, an idea jumped into her head and she stood up. "What if Mike and Tommy get lost in the cave?" she asked. "We can't just leave them there."

"If their bikes are gone, we'll know they got out," said Lulu as she stood up, too. "Let's go look."

"And I'll stay with the ponies," offered Pam.

Anna and Lulu sneaked through the woods back to the cave. They heard Tommy and Mike before they saw them.

"There's no air in my tire!" exclaimed Tommy.

"Maybe you rode over a nail," said Mike.

"In the woods?" said Tommy. "Man, you are dense. Those Pony Pests let the air out."

"It could have been a sharp rock or something," said Mike.

Anna peeked around a bush. Tommy had his hands on his hips and was glaring at Mike. "Why are you defending those stupid girls?" he asked. "And why did you want to follow them, anyway?"

"I didn't want to —" Mike started to say.

"You better know the way back," said Tommy.

"I — uh — guess if we go back to that big trail," said Mike. "And then maybe, uh —"

"Let's go," Lulu whispered in Anna's ear.

They snuck away and reported everything they learned to Pam.

"So Mike and Tommy don't even know the way home," concluded Lulu.

"It's easy to get lost around here," agreed Pam.

"We'd better help them," said Lulu.

Anna looked around at the dense woods surrounding them. Pam and Lulu were right. They had to help the boys — whether they wanted to or not.

Call Me!

The girls led their ponies back to the trail. It went in three directions.

"I wonder which way they went," said Anna.

Acorn turned to the left and sniffed the ground. He took a few steps forward. Anna and Pam exchanged a glance. Sometimes Acorn was an excellent detective.

"Let's follow him," suggested Lulu.

Anna and Acorn led the way. Lulu studied the ground for clues.

"The ground is hard and covered with

leaves here," she said. "Footprints and bike tracks wouldn't show."

Anna put a hand on the whistle hanging around her neck. "Maybe I should blow a signal," she said.

"Good idea," agreed Lulu.

"They won't know it's *us*," said Pam.

"But they'll know it's *someone*," explained Lulu. "Someone who might help them if they're lost."

Anna raised her whistle to her lips and blew three long blasts. The girls and ponies stayed perfectly still and listened. They heard distant voices shouting in reply. Boys' voices. But they couldn't make out what they were saying.

Anna blew her whistle again.

They heard the voices again. This time they were closer.

Anna blew one more time.

A minute later, Tommy and Mike came out of the woods pushing their bikes. Twigs and burrs stuck to their sweaters.

They were surprised to see the Pony Pals.

"YOU!" shouted Tommy angrily.

"We — uh — sort of got a little lost," stammered Mike.

Tommy punched Mike in the arm. "WE?" he shouted at Mike. "You're the one who wanted to go that way."

"Sorry," mumbled Mike.

These two guys are pathetic, thought Anna. But we can't leave them in the woods.

"How'd you find us?" asked Mike.

Anna patted Acorn's neck. "Acorn knew where to go," she said. "I guess he remembers Tommy."

Tommy looked away. He didn't like to be reminded that Acorn used to be his pony. Or that he was ever a little kid.

"Do you want us to tell you the way, or not?" asked Lulu.

"Can't we just follow you?" asked Mike.

"We're riding," said Pam. "You can't keep up on foot."

Lulu shifted in the saddle and pulled a little notebook out of her pocket. "I'll draw you a map," she offered.

"Great," said Mike. "Thanks."

Tommy hit him on the arm again.

Mike stood next to Snow White and Lulu while Lulu drew the map. He whispered a thank-you when she handed it to him.

Tommy snatched the map from Mike. "You'll just get us lost again," he said.

Pam nodded to Lulu and Anna. "Let's go," she said. The girls turned their ponies around and rode away from the boys.

"Hey, how do we know this map is right?" Tommy shouted after them.

They ignored him and kept riding.

Mike should have gotten on his bike and left Tommy behind, thought Anna.

The trail narrowed and the three friends moved into single file.

"Move over, move over," shouted a voice behind them. Snow White startled. Lulu struggled to stay in the saddle and calm her pony.

Anna turned and saw Tommy barreling toward them on Mike's bike. The girls pulled their ponies over.

Tommy passed them with a hoot and a holler.

"He left Mike with *his* bike," observed Lulu. "What a creep!"

"Should we wait for Mike?" asked Lulu.

Anna remembered her research paper. She glanced at the sun through the trees. It was already in the west. The day was passing so fast. "I have to get home," she told her friends. "I told my mom."

"I'll go back and make sure Mike has the map," said Lulu. "You two go ahead. I'll catch up."

By the time Anna got home it was three o'clock. A note written in big, printed words was on the kitchen counter. Anna could read it from across the room.

ANNA HARLEY! CALL ME AT THE DINER
THE MOMENT YOU GET HOME!
—YOUR MOTHER

Anna picked up the phone and punched in the diner's number.

"Off-Main Diner," her mother answered in a cheerful voice.

"It's me, Mom," said Anna. "I'm home."

Before Anna could make excuses, her mother began scolding. "No more trail rides until your paper is done!" she said in a not-very-cheerful voice. "And no drawing for that contest. And *no* hanging out with your Pony Pals, either." She went on and on.

Anna finally slipped in a few words. "I'll do it now, Mom," she said. "I promise."

As soon as Anna hung up the phone, it rang again. It was Pam.

"I just saw Mike pushing Tommy's bike down Riddle Road," she said. "I brought out an air pump and filled the tire for him. I told him he should keep Tommy's bike."

"He wouldn't dare," said Anna.

"I know," agreed Pam. "Hey, let's meet at the diner. You can show Lulu and me your ideas for Ponies on Parade. I can't wait to see them."

"I can't," said Anna. "I have to work on my paper."

"On the surprise subject," teased Pam. "I thought maybe you were finished."

"I haven't *started*," admitted Anna. "I'm grounded until I do it. And I definitely can't try out for painting a pony."

"You *have* to enter the contest," protested Pam.

"Well, I can't," said Anna. "My mom said."

"I'll help you with the paper," offered Pam. "Lulu, too."

"Nobody can help me," said Anna sadly. "I don't have any ideas. I can't read that well. And I hate to write."

"That's because you're dyslexic," said Pam. "But you can still do it, Anna. It's not *impossible*. It's just another Pony Pal Problem we can solve together."

"It's not a Pony Pal Problem," protested Anna. "It's *my* problem. It's my problem with my stupid, dumb brain. And the Pony Pals can't fix that."

Pony Pal E-mail

Anna went to her room and turned on the computer. First she had to choose a subject. It had to be something that was part of her daily life.

Okay, I'll write about computers, she decided. Computers will be my subject.

The second step in the assignment was to do research. Anna went on to the Internet and did a search on the word *computer*. There were hundreds of entries. She stared at the screen.

Which ones should I pick? she wondered. Will I understand what I read?

Suddenly, Anna's e-mail account flashed that she had mail. She opened her inbox and saw that she had two messages. One was from Lulu. The other was from Pam. Both messages had the same subject: PONY PAL E-MAIL MEETING.

She opened Lulu's message first.

We have to pull together and solve this problem. Here's my idea:
Pam and I will help you. Don't be ⊗.
P.S. Don't give up on painting a pony.

The second e-mail was from Pam.

Anna,
Here's my idea for solving our Pony Pal Problem:
Make a list of what you are interested in. Send it to me.
Do it now!

Anna smiled to herself. Pam could be so bossy.

So what am I interested in? Anna asked herself. That was an easy question to answer. She clicked "Reply" and Pam's e-mail address popped into the "To" box.

To: Pam Crandal
cc: Lulu Sanders
Re: Pony Pal E-mail Meeting
   I am interested in:
   Ponies
   Horses
   Drawing
   Nature
   Badd Brook
   Cooking
   — Anna☺

Within a minute, an e-mail came back from Pam.

Ponies is a good subject. But it is too big of an idea. How about Shetland ponies?

Next step: Look up Shetland ponies on the Internet.

I already know a lot about Shetlands, thought Anna. And I can learn more online.

Anna found an article about the history of Shetland ponies. Another article explained their anatomy. There was even a website address for the Shetland Islands. Anna remembered that Shetland ponies came from the Shetland Islands.

She printed out five articles and carefully put a paper clip on each one. Then she sat on her bed to read.

As Anna looked at the first line of the first article, the letters moved on the page like ants. Was that word "mine" or "mind"? And in the next sentence, was it "ride" or "died"? Why couldn't she remember what words looked like?

Anna counted the pages she had printed out. Thirty-six! She had thirty-six pages to read, and she couldn't even make sense of the first line on the first page. Her head was spinning. It was so hard to read. I feel like I have to get outside, she thought. I have to see Acorn.

Anna's mother was coming up the stairs as Anna was going down. "I was just going up to check on you," Mrs. Harley said. "How's the paper coming along?"

"I'm writing about Shetland ponies," Anna reported. "I've been doing research."

Mrs. Harley patted Anna's shoulder. "Good," she said. "And come straight home after school tomorrow. No hanging out with your friends."

"I know," said Anna.

"I'm sorry you can't try out for Ponies on Parade," her mother continued. "If you'd started this assignment two weeks ago —"

"I know," said Anna. She ran out of the house and all the way to the paddock. She hoped, for once, Acorn wouldn't play "hard to catch."

Anna opened the gate and called her pony's name into the dark night. Acorn came

right to her. Tears filled Anna's eyes as she flung her arms around his warm neck.

"Oh, Acorn," she cried. "Why is reading so hard for me?" Tears streamed down her face. Acorn nudged her shoulder with his head. She looked up at him. He licked her tears away.

The next morning, Lulu and Anna walked to school together as usual. They met Pam at the school bus.

"How's your paper?" Pam asked Anna as they walked into school together.

"Great," answered Anna. "Thanks for all the help."

She didn't tell her friends that she couldn't read what she printed out.

During school, four kids and two teachers asked Anna if she was entering the Ponies on Parade contest. A lot of people at school knew she was a good artist. She told them all the same thing. "I'm too busy."

After school, the Pony Pals walked out together. The sun was still bright and the day warm.

"I can't ride today," she told Lulu and Pam. "I have to finish my paper."

"We're not riding, either," said Lulu.

"How come?" asked Anna.

"We're going to help you with your paper," explained Pam.

"Did you really read all the articles?" asked Lulu.

Anna shook her head.

They crossed the street to the Town Green. "We'll read the articles to you," offered Pam. "You can pick out the main ideas. That's all you'll need for the paper."

"It's due tomorrow," said Anna sadly.

"We know," said Lulu. She grabbed Anna's hand. "So let's hurry."

As the Pony Pals were running across the Town Green, Anna spotted a blur of red. Tommy Rand was racing toward them on his bike. He passed so close that Anna felt the breeze.

"Jerk," mumbled Pam as she took a step back.

"Hey, Tommy," Anna yelled after him. "You have a flat tire."

Tommy screeched to a halt and turned to check his back tire.

"Made you look," shouted Lulu.

When the Pony Pals came into the Harley kitchen, they were still laughing.

Mrs. Harley was standing in the middle of the room with her arms folded. She did not look happy.

Another Idea

"Hi, Mom," said Anna. "I thought you were working at the diner today."

"I am," said Mrs. Harley. "I came home to check on you." She turned to Lulu and Pam. "Anna may not ride today. She has schoolwork."

"Mrs. Harley," Pam said in her most businesslike voice. "Lulu and I would like to help Anna with her paper."

"We're going to read the research on Shetland ponies with her," explained Lulu.

"And help her pick out the main ideas," added Pam.

Mrs. Harley eyed them suspiciously.

"I'll write the paper myself," Anna promised. "They're just going to help."

"That paper *must* be written by the time I get home," said Mrs. Harley. "Do you understand?"

"Yes, ma'am," the three girls answered in unison.

Mrs. Harley went back to the diner. Anna went upstairs for the articles on Shetland ponies, her notebook, and pencil case. Pam poured juice for each of them. Lulu fixed a plate of cookies. A few minutes later the three friends were sitting around the picnic table, ready to work.

Pam read. Lulu helped Anna underline the main ideas. As they completed each article, Anna put the ideas into her own words. Lulu wrote them down.

Suddenly, a big brown-and-black head pushed between Lulu and Anna. Acorn! In a

flash he reached for the cookie plate and picked up two cookies in one bite. Anna saw that the gate to the paddock had swung open.

"That gate was locked," said Anna as she grabbed Acorn's halter.

"Acorn must have unlocked it with his mouth," said Pam as she moved the cookie plate out of Acorn's reach.

Lulu ran over to the paddock so Snow White wouldn't get out, too.

Acorn was licking his lips and sniffing around for more cookies.

"Shetland ponies are very clever," laughed Anna. "I'm going to put that in my paper."

"And some of them like chocolate chip cookies," added Pam.

The girls laughed.

Anna led Acorn back to the paddock. "Shetland ponies can pull loads as heavy as they are," she told her pony. "Your ancestors worked in mines. They were small, like you, so they could fit in the tunnels. And they were strong enough to pull carts piled with coal. I bet you could do that, Acorn." She patted his head. "But I wouldn't want you to. Those ponies in the mines spent years underground."

Acorn looked at Anna as if he understood.

She brushed her hand along his strong wide side. All that history is in you, Acorn, she thought.

An idea flashed into Anna's mind like a bolt of lightning. She gave Acorn a big kiss. "Thank you for the idea, Acorn," she said. She ran back to Pam and Lulu at the picnic table.

"I figured it out," she said excitedly.

"What?" asked Pam.

"How to do the paper *and* the Ponies on Parade application at the same time," said Anna excitedly.

"How?" asked Lulu and Pam in unison.

"Here, I'll show you," said Anna. She pulled a copy of the Ponies on Parade application from her notebook and pointed to the top-view pony outline. "The top will look just like Acorn," she said. "So will the legs, hooves, and belly."

"But what about your paper?" asked Pam. "Your mother said —"

"I'm going to write the paper on the sides of the pony," explained Anna. She looked up at her friends and grinned. "The whole history of Shetland ponies will be written *on* my Shetland pony. I'll call it 'My Pony.' "

"That's a great idea!" said Lulu.

"You should write the paper first," said Pam.

"I know," said Anna. She turned to a clean page in her notebook. "I know exactly what to write. I just told it all to Acorn."

"I'll help you edit it," offered Pam.

"Then we can type it on your computer," added Lulu.

They were almost finished writing the essay, when Mike's six-year-old sister, Rosalie, ran into the yard. Her brother, Mike, rode his bike in behind her. Mrs. Lacey worked long hours at the Green Market. Mike had to baby-sit for his sister a lot. Rosalie Lacey loved her big brother. She also loved ponies, especially Acorn.

Rosalie said hello to Acorn and Snow White. Then she came over to the table to talk to the girls. She wanted to know all about the pony drawings. Mike mumbled, "hi." He only acted mean and stupid when he was with Tommy Rand.

Lulu told Rosalie and Mike how Acorn stole two cookies. They both thought it was pretty funny.

Suddenly, Tommy appeared in the driveway on his bike. Anna quickly closed her notebook. She didn't want Tommy Rand to know about Ponies on Parade. The less Tommy Rand knew, the better.

"Hey," Tommy yelled to Mike. "You coming or not?"

Mike looked around shyly at the Pony Pals. "Can Rosalie stay with you?" he asked. "Just for a little while."

"NO!" said the Pony Pals in unison.

"We're busy," explained Anna.

Mike waved to Tommy. "I have to take care of my sister."

"Loser," sneered Tommy as he peeled away.

"Sorry, Mike," said Pam. "But we've got to concentrate on some school stuff right now."

"Anna's got a great idea for Ponies on Parade," added Lulu.

Anna shot a scolding look at Lulu. She didn't want Mike to know about Ponies on Parade, either.

"Acorn's going to be in a parade?" asked Rosalie.

Pam explained Ponies on Parade to Mike and Rosalie.

Anna showed them the devil pony and the half-striped, half-plaid pony.

Mike thought the devil pony was a terrific idea. "You're a really good artist," he told Anna.

Rosalie thought the half-and-half pony was funny.

Next, Anna explained her Shetland pony idea.

"It'll be like a big Acorn doll!" exclaimed Rosalie.

"*If* I win," said Anna. "That's a big if. . . ." She looked from Rosalie to Mike. "So don't tell anyone about it. Okay?"

"Okay," said Rosalie. She crossed her heart. "I promise."

Anna looked Mike right in the eye. "Especially don't tell Tommy," she said.

"I won't," agreed Mike. "He doesn't care, anyway."

Harry Pony

That evening, Anna worked alone in her room. The final copy of the Ponies on Parade application was on her desk. When her mother came in to check on her, Anna was painting Acorn's black mane on the top view.

"Anna Harley, I told you that you couldn't do that," Mrs. Harley said impatiently.

"I finished my paper already, Mom," said Anna proudly. She handed her mother three neatly typed pages.

Mrs. Harley looked it over. "Why, this is very good," she said. "Did you write it all yourself?"

Anna nodded. "But Pam and Lulu helped," she said. "Acorn helped, too. He gave me the idea for Ponies on Parade."

Her mother leaned over Anna and looked at the application.

"I'm going to write about Shetland ponies on the sides with paint," explained Anna.

"How very clever!" exclaimed Mrs. Harley. "You combined your homework and the Ponies on Parade application." She put a hand on Anna's shoulder. "It looks just like Acorn."

"They might not even choose my idea, Mom," Anna reminded her mother.

"That's true," agreed Mrs. Harley. "But I'm glad you're trying."

Anna stayed up until ten o'clock to finish her application.

On the way to school the next morning, Anna and Lulu stopped at the library. Mr. Remington, the head librarian, was unlocking the door. "What can I do for you young ladies?" he asked.

"Anna has an application for Ponies on Parade," said Lulu.

"Should I give it to you?" asked Anna.

"Certainly," he said. He lowered his voice to a whisper. "I filled one out myself. Mine is called 'Harry Pony.' He looks just like Harry Potter."

"That's a great idea," exclaimed Lulu.

"I hope the judges are of the same opinion," said Mr. Remington. "Your application is the thirty-first entry, Miss Harley."

Thirty-one applications for ten ponies, thought Anna. She'd never get to paint a pony.

"Don't worry, Anna," said Lulu as they walked away from the library. "Your idea is terrific, too."

But Anna did worry. And she worried about her research paper.

On Friday, Mrs. Waters handed them back. Anna got a B-plus.

When the bell rang, the Pony Pals went to their lockers together.

"I got an A," said Lulu. "What did you get, Pam?"

"A-plus," answered Pam.

Anna wasn't surprised that Lulu and Pam both earned A's. They were great students. But she was surprised with her B-plus. It was her best grade yet in Language Arts. Lulu and Pam were looking at her.

"How did you do?" asked Pam.

She grinned and showed them her grade. Mrs. Waters had written, "Good work, Anna!" under it.

"Thanks for helping me," Anna told her friends.

"It was fun," said Pam. "Now we have to

find out who's going to paint the ten ponies."

Lulu put an arm around Anna's shoulder. "I hope one of them is you," she said.

Pam banged her locker shut. "Come on," she said. "Let's go get the newspaper."

The Pony Pals ran all the way to the Green Market. Pam picked up a paper from the rack outside and held it out for Anna.

Anna shook her head. "You look," she said. "I'm too nervous. Besides, you read faster."

Pam checked the index on the first page. *"Ponies on Parade contest,"* she read, *"page ten."* She turned to page ten, found the article, and scanned the list of winners.

Anna held her breath.

Pam looked down the list of names.

"Wilhelmina Wiggins," read Pam. "And *Justin Remington."*

" 'Harry Pony' is such a good idea," said Lulu. "But what about Anna?"

Anna's heart was pounding in her chest. Her mouth was dry.

Pam looked up. Her expression was very

serious. "I'm sorry, Anna," she said, "but I'm afraid that . . . you will have to paint one of those ponies, too."

"I will?" asked Anna, confused.

A grin spread across Pam's face. Lulu jumped up and down and hugged Anna. "Congratulations," she said.

"You have to pick up your art supplies from Klein's Hardware," added Pam.

"Let's do it right now," suggested Lulu.

"I don't even know what I need yet," said Anna. Her heart was still beating fast, but now it was with excitement, not nervousness. She was going to paint a life-size pony and it was going to be on display at the Fall Festival.

"Hi!" shouted a friendly voice. It was Rosalie coming out of the Green Market with Mike. Mike was carrying a bag of groceries.

"Mike's going to make spaghetti for dinner," bragged Rosalie. "Mom said."

"Well, Anna's going to paint one of the ponies," exclaimed Lulu. "She won!"

A grin spread across Mike's face. "Cool," he said. "Where you going to do it?"

"Can we help?" Rosalie begged Mike. "Please."

"Sure," said Mike.

If Mike and Rosalie help, thought Anna, Tommy will come by. And Tommy Rand always means trouble.

"We already have enough people," Anna told Rosalie and Mike.

"But I *want* to," whined Rosalie. "And Mike said I could."

"You can play with Mimi tomorrow," he said. "I have something else to do, anyway."

He's probably got something to do with Tommy, thought Anna. She looked Mike in the eye. "Mike, please don't tell Tommy I'm painting one of the ponies. Okay?"

"I won't," he agreed. "But who cares, anyway?" He took Rosalie's hand and walked away.

Mike's mad I didn't let him and Rosalie help paint the pony, thought Anna. Will he tell Tommy?

Lulu put an arm around Anna's shoulder. "Don't worry about Mike and Tommy," she said. "You won!"

"Let's go to the diner and celebrate," suggested Pam. "We'll make a list of the supplies you need, Anna."

"And tell your mom," added Lulu.

"Okay," agreed Anna.

A few minutes later the girls walked into the diner. "Just in time," Mrs. Harley called to them. "I'm cutting up a pan of brownies."

First, Anna told her mother about the B-plus. Then she told her she was a Ponies on Parade winner. "But I only have a week to do it," she added. "The Fall Festival is next Saturday."

Mrs. Harley gave the girls a plate of brownies. "You don't even have a week," she said. "You have to do it all this weekend."

"What? But —" Anna started to say.

"You have to concentrate on schoolwork during the week," explained Mrs. Harley. "Look what happened with that research paper."

"But the pony is as big as Acorn!" protested Anna.

"You'd better get started, then," said Mrs. Harley.

Pony Pal
Planning Meeting

The girls took the brownies and glasses of milk to their favorite booth.

"How can I paint a pony in two days?" Anna asked as she slid into the booth.

"We'll help you," offered Lulu. "If you tell us what to do."

"Will you write the words on the sides for me?" asked Anna.

"Sure," agreed Pam as she reached for a brownie. "That's a good way for us to help."

"But now it's time for a Pony Pal Planning Meeting," said Lulu.

"A Pony Pal Ponies on Parade Planning Meeting," added Anna with a giggle.

Pam opened her notebook and they made a list of the supplies they would need.

THE PONY PAL PLAN FOR PAINTING A PONY
SUPPLIES
PAINTS
Tan
Light yellow
Black
Dark pink
White

BRUSHES
2 wide
2 midsize
4 narrow
Drop cloth
Newspapers
Can of brush cleaner
Paper towels

Next, the girls made a schedule for the next two days.

"We can't neglect our ponies," said Lulu.

"We'll take short trail rides," suggested Pam.

"But we have to spend most of our time on the painted pony," added Anna.

"It's going to take a really long time," added Lulu.

The Pony Pals worked on the schedule until they were all happy with it.

SCHEDULE

SATURDAY

8:30 A.M.	Pick up supplies at Klein's Hardware
9–12	Paint pony
12–12:30 P.M.	Lunch
12:30–3	Groom and ride the real ponies
3–6	Paint pony

SUNDAY

9 A.M.–12	Paint pony
12 P.M.–1	Exercise real ponies on Pony Pal Trail
1–2	Ride to diner for brunch
2–6	Paint pony

The next morning Pam rode Lightning to Anna's. She put her pony in the paddock with the other ponies, and the girls walked over to Klein's Hardware for supplies. When they got back to Anna's, they put them out on the picnic table. At nine o'clock a big truck rolled into the driveway. Two men carried a life-size white fiberglass pony into the yard.

"It already looks like Acorn," observed Pam. "It's shaped like a Shetland pony."

"You're right," agreed Anna. "It's almost as big as Acorn, too." She ran her hand over the smooth white surface. She felt scared. The pony was bigger than anything she'd ever painted.

Acorn stood at the paddock fence and nickered as if to say, "What's that pony doing here?"

Anna went over to him. He nuzzled her shoulder.

"It's not a real pony," she explained. "But I hope it will look like one when we're done. I'll need your help, Acorn. You're my model."

Lightning and Snow White weren't interested in the pretend pony. But Acorn stayed at the fence.

"What do we do first?" Pam asked Anna.

"We'll paint the body tan," she instructed.

"Except for where the writing goes," put in Pam.

The girls worked hard all morning.

After lunch they went for a short trail ride. They were back at work when Tommy Rand rode into the yard on his bicycle.

"Look at the Pony Pests playing with the big pony doll!" he laughed. He rode a circle around the girls and model pony. "Isn't that cute?"

Mike rode into the yard behind Tommy. But he stopped his bike and got off without saying anything.

"Go away!" Anna told Tommy.

"Go away!" mimicked Tommy.

Anna turned to Mike. "You said you wouldn't tell him!" she said.

"You said you wouldn't tell him!" repeated Tommy.

Tommy did a good imitation of Anna, which made her even angrier.

"Stop it!" she shouted at him.

"Leave us alone," added Lulu.

Tommy kept riding around the girls and the half-painted pony. "Stop it," he shouted in his Anna voice. "Leave us alone," he added in a Lulu voice.

"You shouldn't have let the air out of his tire," Mike mumbled to Anna.

"Well, you shouldn't have told him," Anna shot back at Mike.

"Well, you shouldn't have told him," repeated Tommy.

Anna put down her paintbrush and took a deep breath. Getting angry wasn't helping. What could she say that Tommy wouldn't repeat?

"But Tommy, you love ponies," Anna said in a sweet voice. "Remember when Acorn was your pony? We saw those great pictures

of you and Acorn in the parade."

Tommy slowed down and glared at her. But he didn't repeat what she said.

"And you were so *cute* in that teddy bear costume for the parade," added Pam.

Tommy regained his balance and sped toward the driveway. "Later for you, Pests."

"Later for you, Pests!" Anna shouted after him.

Mike got on his bike to follow Tommy. "You'll be sorry," he said over his shoulder.

The three girls looked at one another. Lulu was the first to speak. "Now Mike's mad at us, too," she said.

"Well, I'm really mad at Mike," said Anna. "He shouldn't have told Tommy we were painting a pony."

Pam dipped her brush in black paint. "We don't have time to be angry," she said. "We have to keep working." She went back to writing on the pony's side.

Mike and Tommy didn't bother the Pony Pals again that day. But Anna was worried. Tommy and Mike wouldn't be happy until they got back at the girls.

* * *

By Sunday night, the painted pony was finished. Anna's parents and Lulu's grandmother came out to admire it.

"So lifelike," said Grandmother Sanders. "From a distance I thought it was Acorn."

"The essay on Shetlands is interesting," added Mr. Harley. "Folks will learn a lot about these ponies."

Acorn was standing at the fence, watching. He whinnied as if to say, "Hey, over here. I'm the *real* pony."

They all laughed and went over to give him attention.

After school Monday, Anna noticed Acorn's eyes were a little bit darker than the painted pony's. She made the painted pony's eyes darker.

Wednesday after school she observed that Acorn's black mane looked golden in the sunlight. She added some gold streaks to the painted pony's mane.

Thursday night Anna said good night to

Acorn. She glanced over at the painted pony. She wondered who would buy it.

Before breakfast on Friday morning, Anna went out to feed Acorn. Lulu was already outside. But she wasn't in the paddock. She was running across the yard toward Anna.

"Look!" Lulu shouted, pointing at My Pony.

Anna looked toward her painted pony.

It was covered with red paint marks. She ran closer. Her heart beat angrily in her chest. Red letters were painted all over My Pony. They all spelled the same thing: ML WAS HERE.

The Note

Anna and Lulu walked around the graffiti-covered painted pony.

Acorn whinnied as if to say, "What happened to my play friend?"

Half-sad, half-angry tears flowed down Anna's cheeks. "It's *ruined!*" she wailed. "I will never, *ever* forgive Mike Lacey."

Lulu brushed her hand down the ML WAS HERE on the pony's nose. "We'd better feed our ponies," she told Anna. "Or we'll be late for school."

Anna and Lulu were waiting for Pam when

she got off the school bus. They told her the bad news.

"I want to turn Mike Lacey in to the police!" said Anna. "He destroyed private property. His mother is going to have a *fit* and it will serve him right."

"Maybe Tommy did it," said Pam.

"Of course he did," said Anna. "The two of them."

"But maybe *just* Tommy did it," continued Pam. "Maybe Mike doesn't know anything about it."

"Mike was mad at us, too," protested Anna. "Remember? He said, 'You'll be sorry.' I'm sure he's in on it." She glared at the school bike racks. "Those guys ride their bikes to school. I'm waiting for them out here."

Lulu put a hand on her arm. "Hold it," she said. "I have an idea. You accuse Mike. I'll watch how he reacts. Pam, you watch Tommy. How they look and act can tell us a lot."

"Okay," Anna agreed. "But I still think Mike did it."

As the girls were walking to the bike rack, Mike and Tommy rode into the school yard.

"Mike Lacey," Anna shouted before he even got off his bike. "You are going to regret what you did to that pony for the rest of your life!"

Mike screeched to a halt in front of Anna. "What?" he asked. He looked confused. "What happened?"

The bell rang for the beginning of school.

Anna kicked his bike wheel. "You know what I'm talking about," she hissed. "Your initials are all over my pony. 'ML was here.' Does that sound familiar?"

"All over Acorn?" he asked, confused. He looked at Tommy.

Tommy was twisting his mouth.

Tommy's trying not to laugh, thought Anna.

"What did you do?" Mike asked Tommy.

The principal walked into the middle of the group of five. "Break it up," he ordered. "No more chatting. Rand, Lacey, you go in first.

Now hustle." He followed them all into school.

Anna wanted to run after the boys, but Lulu held her back.

"We have to save your painted pony," said Lulu. "That's what's most important."

"It will take *forever*," wailed Anna. "We don't have time."

"We'll stay up all night if we have to," said Lulu.

"We can't paint it in the dark," protested Anna. She swallowed back tears. They'd all worked so hard and the pony had looked so wonderful.

"We can do it in your garage," suggested Lulu. "Your dad can park his truck outside."

"We stayed up all night with sick ponies, swans, and missing hamsters," Pam reminded them. "We can stay up all night for the messed-up pony."

"It's sort of the same thing," agreed Lulu.

Ms. Waters was standing by the door to

their classroom. "Are you three joining us to-day?" she asked.

"Yes, Ms. Waters," they answered in unison. They went into the classroom and took their seats.

It was the longest school day of Anna's life. When three o'clock finally came, the Pony Pals rushed out of the building. An eighth grader stopped them in the doorway and handed Anna a note.

The three girls huddled and Anna opened the paper.

Anna,
I'm sorry about what happened to the painted pony. I didn't know anything about it until you told me. You should try to paint over what Tommy wrote. I can help you. Rosalie is going to Mimi's after school, so I don't have to baby-sit.
See you later.
Mike

"I told you he didn't have anything to do

with it," said Pam.

"Maybe he didn't," agreed Anna. "But I don't want him to help."

"But Anna," protested Pam. "We need all the help we can get."

"Okay, he can help," agreed Anna. "But if Tommy Rand bothers us, I'm throwing paint all over his bike. And it won't be red."

The girls moved the pony into the garage. They were setting out the paints when Mike came in. When he saw the graffiti-covered pony, his mouth dropped open.

"Your pal Tommy Rand did this," said Anna.

"I know," said Mike.

Mike must be angry with Tommy, too, thought Anna.

The Pony Pals and Mike worked with small brushes to cover up the red paint. It was difficult to do and took a long time. At seven o'clock Mrs. Harley sent them fried chicken dinners from the diner. They took a short break to eat and went right back to work.

Mike had to leave at midnight. But the girls worked until they were done. It was 1:30 in the morning. Anna locked My Pony in the garage. The real ponies were asleep in the paddock. Snow White's coat glowed in the moonlight.

"It's a clear night," observed Lulu. "We'll have good weather tomorrow for the festival."

"I wonder if anyone will buy My Pony," said Anna as they walked into the house.

"I know who *should* buy it," said Pam.

Pam and Lulu exchanged a glance and burst out laughing. They both had the same idea.

"That's the perfect person," said Lulu.

"Who?" asked Anna.

Pam whispered a name to Anna. She smiled at her best friends. It was a great idea. They *had* thought of the perfect person to buy My Pony. Anna only hoped that it would work.

My Pony

At nine o'clock the next morning, the girls and Mr. Harley carried My Pony to the center of the Town Green. Angel Pony, Tuxedo Pony, Patriotic Pony, and Harry Pony were already there. They were soon joined by Glitter Pony, Little Red Riding Pony, Unicorn Pony, Baseball Pony, and Sky Pony.

By ten o'clock, ten painted ponies were lined up in the center of the Town Green. Ms. Wiggins came over to take a close look at My Pony. She congratulated Anna on a fine job.

"I couldn't have done it without Pam and Lulu," Anna told her.

"And Mike," added Lulu.

Anna told Ms. Wiggins what had happened to My Pony.

"Mike would never do something like that," protested Ms. Wiggins. She liked Mike Lacey. "Besides, he helped you fix it."

"I know," agreed Anna. "But sometimes Tommy gets him to do lots of stuff he shouldn't do."

Ms. Wiggins smiled and waved. "There's Mike now," she said.

Mike and Rosalie walked over to them. Rosalie grabbed Anna's hand. "Can I help you give pony rides?" she asked. "Please?"

"Sure," said Anna.

Mike Lacey checked out My Pony. "It looks great!" he said.

"Thanks for helping," Anna said.

Ms. Wiggins held up her camera. "I'll take a picture of you with the pony," she offered.

Anna put an arm around the painted pony's neck. Ms. Wiggins took two shots.

"Let's get a picture with Pam and Lulu because they helped," said Anna.

Lulu and Pam ran over to get in the picture.

Anna motioned for Mike to join them. "You helped, too, Mike," she said.

The four friends stood near My Pony and smiled for the camera.

The Town Green was now full of people. The town band played loud, cheerful music in the bandstand. Dr. and Mrs. Crandal operated a booth for Toss the Ring. There were a lot of games and prizes. Lulu's grandmother painted faces.

St. Francis Animal Shelter had a booth. They were trying to find homes for two litters of kittens, a dog, and a potbellied pig. Anna's mother ran the food tent. Mr. Harley and two other volunteer firemen cooked at the huge charcoal grill. Tommy and Mike were hanging out together.

As Anna led a little girl around the pony ride ring, she spotted Mike and Tommy.

When Anna saw them, they were tossing hoops at bottles.

At one o'clock the Pony Pals took a break. They bought lunch from the food tent and sat under a maple tree to eat. Anna sat where she could see her painted pony. Soon My Pony would be auctioned off. She might never see it again.

Mrs. Rand — Tommy's mother — was the only person standing near My Pony. She was running a hand over its back and smiling. The Pony Pals liked Mrs. Rand. They felt sorry for her because she had Tommy for a son. But Mrs. Rand didn't seem to mind. And mostly, Anna had noticed, Tommy behaved around his mother.

"Do you really think Mrs. Rand will buy it?" asked Anna with a giggle.

"She might do it for Tommy," answered Pam.

"That would be so perfect!" exclaimed Anna.

Lulu stood up. "It's time to talk to her,"

she said. The Pony Pals walked over to Mrs. Rand.

"Anna Harley," said Mrs. Rand excitedly. "This is a perfect copy of Acorn. Absolutely perfect. Acorn was such a good pony." She sighed. "I miss him."

"I think Tommy misses Acorn, too," said Lulu sadly.

"He talks about Acorn sometimes," added Pam.

Mrs. Rand's eyes filled with tears. "I'm so glad you told me that. Tommy's growing up so fast," she said. "Sometimes I don't recognize my sweet little boy."

Anna put a hand on My Pony's head. "Maybe you should buy My Pony at the auction," she said. "Then Tommy can always remember his time with Acorn."

"And you'll be giving money to the fire department," added Lulu.

"Why, that's a perfect idea," said Mrs. Rand enthusiastically. "I'd put it on the front lawn."

"Tommy will be so happy," agreed Anna. She saw a line of kids waiting for pony rides.

"We have to go back and do more pony rides," said Pam. "There's a big line of kids."

The girls said good-bye to Mrs. Rand and headed back to the riding ring.

"Look at Mr. Show-off," said Lulu.

Tommy Rand was riding his unicycle around the Town Green. People stopped to watch him do tricks.

"I hate that he's so good at that," commented Anna.

Just then, Tommy noticed the Pony Pals. He rode right over to them. "That pony thing you painted looks dumb," he said.

"Is that why you tried to ruin it?" asked Pam.

"ML did that," said Tommy with a wink. He pedaled off.

Lulu and Anna exchanged a glance. Tommy was in for a big surprise.

At three o'clock, people gathered around the bandstand. The Pony Pals stood behind the crowd with their real ponies. The band played a fanfare and the auctioneer, Mr. Chambers, stepped forward.

Anna looked around for Mrs. Harley. She was standing up front with Ms. Wiggins and Pam's mother. Rosalie stayed with the Pony Pals. Mike hung around nearby.

"Hey there, Mr. Rand," the auctioneer called out. "Help me out here."

Tommy circled his unicycle around to face the auctioneer.

"I need two big boys to carry the ponies up front for me," he explained. "Someone help Mr. Rand. Let's go."

Tommy motioned for Mike to help him. The two of them carried Harry Pony to the front. Mr. Chambers told them to stand beside the pony.

The band played a fanfare again. "First pony. Harry Pony," announced Mr. Chambers.

The principal of Wiggins Elementary bought Harry Pony as a gift for the school. Mrs. Baxter, the real estate agent in town, bought Angel Pony. "It'll look great in our field," she said into the mike. A woman the girls didn't know bought Patriotic Pony.

My Pony was the last pony to be auctioned off. Mike and Tommy carried it up front.

The auctioneer said that Acorn was the model for My Pony. Many people turned and smiled at Anna and Acorn.

"And who will start the bidding?" asked the auctioneer.

Mrs. Rand made the first bid.

Tommy looked stunned.

Mr. Olson raised Mrs. Rand's bid. The real Acorn came from Mr. Olson's horse farm. Anna liked Mr. Olson a lot. But she still wanted Mrs. Rand to buy My Pony.

Mrs. Rand bid higher.

So did Mr. Olson.

Anna crossed her fingers.

Tommy shifted nervously from foot to foot.

Mrs. Rand went even higher.

No one else made a bid.

"Going, going, gone!" shouted the auction-eer with a bang of the gavel.

Mrs. Rand went up to the bandstand. She was smiling and looking around at the audience. The auctioneer handed her the microphone.

"Acorn was my son Tommy's pony," Mrs. Rand told the audience. "He's missed him." She smiled down at Tommy, who was standing beside My Pony. "Now he'll always have Acorn." She waved to Anna. "Thank you, Anna Harley, for taking such good care of Acorn and making such a wonderful copy of him."

Everyone clapped.

The Pony Pals exchanged a glance, grinned, and joined the applause. Tommy and Mrs. Rand were surrounded by friends congratulating them.

Anna led Acorn over to My Pony. It was time to say good-bye. Acorn sniffed the fake pony's face. Anna gave My Pony a quick hug. Acorn nickered as if to say, "Hey, what about me?"

She threw her arms around Acorn's neck. "You're my real and only pony," she said.

Do you love ponies? Don't miss the final

Pony Pals®

adventure!

Super Special #6: *The Last Pony Ride*

Lulu looked around the yard. It was good to be back in Wiggins with her Pony Pals. Then she remembered she wasn't going to stay in Wiggins. Her father was going to be working in Botswana, Africa, for two years, and he wanted her to live with him.

It had seemed like a good idea when she was there. But when she thought about telling Anna and Pam the news, she felt nervous and sad. I'll do it now, she decided. She looked around the yard. "Where's Pam?" she asked.

"Pam had to take care of Starfire," explained Anna. "She said we should go there when you wake up. I'm so glad you're home."

"Me, too," agreed Lulu. She smiled, but she didn't feel happy.

95

Even when she was riding Snow White, Lulu didn't feel happy. She would be leaving her Pony Pals and her pony again. Only this time she was leaving for good.

A tear trickled down Lulu's cheek. She loved her father and wanted to live with him. And she loved being around the big animals in Africa, especially the elephants. But how could she leave her Pony Pals? How could she leave Snow White?

"It's so great to be Pony Pals again," Anna called over her shoulder.

It sure is, Lulu thought as she rode Snow White over the familiar trail. I love my Pony Pals.

The first thing the girls did at Pam's place was take care of their ponies. Then Pam brought them to see Starfire in his stall. Starfire belonged to Mrs. Crandall's friend Eleanor. Eleanor used to jump with the horse in Olympic competitions, but Starfire strained a tendon and wouldn't be able to compete anymore. Eleanor had asked Pam and her mother to take care of Starfire and make sure he got a lot of exercise.

Pam was still talking about Starfire as the girls headed to the house for dinner.

Lulu hadn't told her Pony Pals that she was moving to Botswana yet. She had to tell them. Now was the time. Her heart pounded in her chest.

"I'm going back to Africa," she blurted out. "I'm going to live there. With my father."

"What?" exclaimed Pam.

"Africa?" said Anna.

Lulu told them the whole story. How her father was going to write a book about elephants. That people spoke English in Botswana and there was a school she could go to and her dad had an apartment. She'd be going on camping trips with her dad, too—in the camping jeep. She couldn't bring Snow White.

"You can't just leave," protested Anna. "We're the Pony Pals."

"But my dad—" said Lulu.

"Do you want to go?" asked Anna.

"No," said Lulu softly. "I want to stay here."

"Did you tell him you didn't want to move to Africa?" asked Pam.

Lulu shook her head. "It seemed like an okay idea when I was there," she said. "He's my dad. I missed him."

"He'll still come to see you sometimes," said Pam.

"And you can go visit him again," added Anna.

"I didn't think about that," admitted Lulu. She looked at her friends. "I don't want to leave."

"This is a Pony Pal Problem," said Pam, "and we have to solve it."

Tears filled Anna's eyes. "We have to save the Pony Pals," she said. "And we will."

Dear Reader,

I am having fun researching and writing the Pony Pal books. I've met great kids and wonderful ponies at homes, farms, and riding schools. Some of my ideas for Pony Pal adventures have even come from these visits.

I remember the day I made up the main characters for the series. I was walking on a country road in New England. First, I decided that the three girls would be smart, independent, and kind. Then I gave them their names—Pam, Anna, and Lulu. (Look at the initial of each girl's name. See what it spells when you put them together.) Later, I created the three ponies. When I reached home, I turned on my computer and started to write. And I haven't stopped since!

My friends say that I am a little bit like all of the Pony Pals. I am very organized, like Pam. I love nature, like Lulu. But I think that I am most like Anna. I am dyslexic and a good artist, just like her.

Readers often wonder about my life. I live in an apartment in New York City near Central Park and the Museum of Natural History. I enjoy swimming, hiking, painting, and reading. I also love to make up stories. I have been writing novels for children and young adults for more than twenty years! Several of my books have won the Children's Choice Award. To learn more, visit my Web site: www.jeannebetancourt.com.

Many Pony Pal readers send me letters, drawings, and photos. I tape them to the wall in my office. They inspire me to write more Pony Pal stories. Thank you very much!

I don't ride anymore and I've never had a pony. But you don't have to ride to love ponies! And you certainly don't need a pony to be a Pony Pal.

Happy Reading,

Jeanne Betancourt

P.S. There are other Pony Pal books where the Pony Pals have to solve a problem caused by Tommy Rand and Mike Lacey, including: #20: STOLEN PONIES, #23: THE PONY AND THE BEAR, #34: THE PONY AND THE LOST SWAN, and #36: THE PONY AND THE HAUNTED BARN.

In Pony Pals #2: A PONY FOR KEEPS, Anna's parents say she can't keep Acorn because of her low grades in school.

MORE SERIES YOU'LL FALL IN LOVE WITH

Gabi is a lucky girl. She can speak English *and* Spanish. But some days, when things get crazy, Gabi's words get all mixed-up!

In a family of superstars, it's hard to stand out. But Abby is about to surprise her friends, her family, and most of all, herself!

Ghostville Elementary™

Welcome to Sleepy Hollow Elementary! Everyone says the basement is haunted, but no one's ever gone downstairs to prove it. Until now...

This year, Jeff and Cassidy's classroom is moving to the basement—the creepy, haunted basement. And you thought your school was scary...?

Learn more at www.scholastic.com/books
Available Wherever Books Are Sold.

Heartland™

Share Every Moment...

❏ BFF	0-439-13020-4	#1: Coming Home	$4.99 US
❏ BFF	0-439-13022-0	#2: After the Storm	$4.99 US
❏ BFF	0-439-13024-7	#3: Breaking Free	$4.99 US
❏ BFF	0-439-13025-5	#4: Taking Chances	$4.99 US
❏ BFF	0-439-13026-3	#5: Come What May	$4.99 US
❏ BFF	0-439-13035-2	#6: One Day You'll Know	$4.99 US
❏ BFF	0-439-31714-2	#7: Out of the Darkness	$4.99 US
❏ BFF	0-439-31715-0	#8: Thicker Than Water	$4.99 US
❏ BFF	0-439-31716-9	#9: Every New Day	$4.99 US
❏ BFF	0-439-31717-7	#10: Tomorrow's Promise	$4.99 US
❏ BFF	0-439-33967-7	#11: True Enough	$4.99 US
❏ BFF	0-439-33968-5	#12: Sooner or Later	$4.99 US

Available wherever you buy books, or use this order form.

Scholastic Inc., P.O. Box 7502, Jefferson City, MO 65102

Please send me the books I have checked above. I am enclosing $_____ (please add $2.00 to cover shipping and handling). Send check or money order — no cash or C.O.D.s please.

Name_____ Birth date_____

Address_____

City_____ State/Zip_____

Please allow four to six weeks for delivery. Offer good in U.S.A. only. Sorry, mail orders are not available to residents of Canada. Prices subject to change.

www.scholastic.com/kids

SCHOLASTIC

HLBL903

THE SECRETS OF DROON

A Magical Series by Tony Abbott

Under the stairs, a magical world awaits you!

- ❑ BDK 0-590-10839-5   #1: The Hidden Stairs and the Magic Carpet
- ❑ BDK 0-590-10841-7   #2: Journey to the Volcano Palace
- ❑ BDK 0-590-10840-9   #3: The Mysterious Island
- ❑ BDK 0-590-10842-5   #4: City in the Clouds
- ❑ BDK 0-590-10843-3   #5: The Great Ice Battle
- ❑ BDK 0-590-10844-1   #6: The Sleeping Giant of Goll
- ❑ BDK 0-439-18297-2   #7: Into the Land of the Lost
- ❑ BDK 0-439-18298-0   #8: The Golden Wasp
- ❑ BDK 0-439-20772-X   #9: The Tower of the Elf King
- ❑ BDK 0-439-20784-3   #10: Quest for the Queen
- ❑ BDK 0-439-20785-1   #11: The Hawk Bandits of Tarkoom
- ❑ BDK 0-439-20786-X   #12: Under the Serpent Sea
- ❑ BDK 0-439-30606-X   #13: The Mask of Maliban
- ❑ BDK 0-439-30607-8   #14: Voyage of the *Jaffa Wind*
- ❑ BDK 0-439-30608-6   #15: The Moon Scroll
- ❑ BDK 0-439-30609-4   #16: The Knights of Silversnow
- ❑ BDK 0-439-42078-4   #17: Dream Thief
- ❑ BDK 0-439-42079-2   #18: Search for the Dragon Ship

$3.99 each!

- ❑ BDK 0-439-42077-6   Special Edition #1: The Magic Escapes $4.99

Available Wherever You Buy Books or Use This Order Form

www.scholastic.com

❚❚ **SCHOLASTIC**

SODBL80